In the City

by Robyn Silbey
illustrated by Mordicai Gerstein

Scott Foresman

Editorial Offices: Glenview, Illinois • New York, New York
Sales Offices: Reading, Massachusetts • Duluth, Georgia
Glenview, Illinois • Carrollton, Texas • Menlo Park, California

I like going to the city.
It is busy everywhere.

On the streets and on the
sidewalks, cars and people,
here and there.

People coming, people going,
dashing, dashing up and down.

Cars are coming, trucks
are going, moving fast around
the town.

In the city, moms and dads
go off to work both near and far.

In the city, children go off to
school by bus and car.

What has happened in the city?

Cars and people everywhere!

No one is dashing.
No one is running.

No one is moving anywhere!

No cars are moving.
No trucks are moving.

No vans are moving,
here or there.

What has happened in the city?

What made it stop?
What could it be?

Three little dogs are in the city.
They are having fun like you
and me!